# ANARA'S MELODIC TRAIL

**Anara's Melodic Trail**
**Nisha Thayil Manglani**

All rights reserved
Copyright © 2023 by Nisha Thayil Manglani

No part of this publication may be reproduced, distributed, or transmitted in any form or by any means, including photocopying, recording, or other electronic or mechanical methods, without the prior written permission of the publisher, except in the case of brief quotations embodied in critical reviews and certain other noncommercial uses permitted by copyright law.

This is a work of fiction. Names, characters, places and incidents either are products of the author's imagination or are used fictitiously. Any resemblance to actual events or locales or persons, living or dead, is entirely coincidental.

Published by BooxAi

ISBN: 978-965-578-155-7

# Anara's Melodic Trail

Nisha Thayil Manglani

Illustrated by
Nisha Thayil Manglani

I begin by expressing my heartfelt appreciation to my incredible husband for his unwavering support throughout this project. From reading early drafts to meticulously editing every word in this piece, his invaluable input has transformed it into the truly special book it has become.

I am also immensely grateful to our two daughters, whose limitless creativity and unwavering support have been the driving force behind my book. They have consistently served as my greatest inspiration.

I extend my warmest wishes to you all both parents and children. May this story, poem, and my love for music not only bring you joy but also serve as a wellspring of inspiration, igniting your imagination and motivating you to pursue your own creative endeavors. May the words and verses intertwine, creating a tapestry of melodies, rhythms, and emotions that deeply resonate with you, immersing you in the captivating beauty and passion of a musical world.

Once upon a time, in the city of Harmony, there lived a spirited girl named Anara. Raindrops fell gently from the sky, creating a soothing rhythm on the rooftops. Anara's heart was filled with an immense love for music, and she couldn't contain her excitement. Everywhere she went, whether it was passing by the majestic trees or visiting the bustling carnival, music seemed to dance in her thoughts. Even the gentle breeze at the beach carried with it the enchanting melodies she adored. But on this particular rainy day, Anara had a special request for her Mom.

With a sparkle in her eyes, she asked, "Mummy, Mummy, can I show you where I see melodies, tunes, and sing all my songs?" she eagerly asked, unable to contain her enthusiasm.
Anara's Mom matched her daughter's energy with equal excitement. With a wide smile, she replied, "Absolutely! Take me there, my sweet pea! Lead the way, and let's discover the magical places where music comes alive together!"

So Anara took her Mom on a dreamy melodic trail through the farm, beach, carnival and all around merrily!
Piano TRAIL

"Look, Mummy! I see a farm!" Anara exclaimed with delight, pointing towards the sprawling fields and colorful barns in the distance.

Anara's Mom's curiosity was piqued as she leaned in and asked, "Oh my! What do you see in the farm, my little explorer? Tell me all about it!"

I see music in the trees
I see music in the butterfly's, the sheep
And in the cows
And in the farm breeze

Mummy can I take you to my garden!
Let's go!
Garden of
D.C.al Fine
I see music everywhere
Singing through the garden,
The fence, the plants, the birds
And in the leaves with every breath.

"Mummy, Mummy, come to my school! I want to show you what I see!" Anara exclaimed, brimming with energy and anticipation.

Anara's Mom couldn't help but smile at her daughter's enthusiasm. "Of course, my dear! I would love to see the world through your eyes. Lead the way, and let's discover the wonders of your school together!" she replied warmly.

Mummy,
I see music in my school
In the mountains,
And In the windows
Bouncing all around the street

Sounds so magical, exclaimed Anara's Mummy.

"Mummy, Mummy, look!" Anara exclaimed, pulling her Mom's hand and pointing towards a familiar sight. "Wait, this place looks familiar! It's our house!" Anara's mom giggled, recognizing their beloved home.

Anara joined in the laughter, her eyes sparkling with delight. "Yes, Mummy! Our house is filled with music too. Let me show you the melodies that fill every corner!"

Hand in hand, they entered their home, ready to explore the familiar yet magical world where their own unique symphony awaited.

I see music in my home
Dancing in my backyard
Playing the best song
Oh I can see music in my city
Playing the most beautiful chords
On this baby grand with such power and force!

"Mummy, do you want to go somewhere relaxing?" Anara asked, her eyes shining with anticipation.

"Absolutely, my love!" Anara's Mummy replied with a smile. "Let's go to the beach, where the gentle waves and sandy shores bring tranquility."

As they arrived at the beach, Anara's Mummy marveled at the vastness of the ocean. "Wow! What do you see here, my dear?" she asked, curious to discover the beach's magic through Anara's eyes.

I see music at the beach
In the tabla, and in the sitar
I see music moving with the waves
And the tides, swishing Side to side
As the octopus says hello
With a musical smile
The sun comes up
And it tells me lets take a dive and listen to the sweet cello!

"Mummy, do you want to do something fun?" Anara asked, her face beaming with excitement.
"Oh my! There's more?" Anara's Mom exclaimed, surprised by the suggestion.
"Yes, Mummy! Let me show you what I see at the carnival!" Anara replied eagerly, tugging at her mom's hand and leading her towards the lively and colorful world of the carnival.

I see music la la la la La
Makes me sing, sing so endlessly
Oh I hear the drum beat
It's as loud as the crowd in a circus
Oh the slides, the rides,
the popcorn and shows
I see the music
In every single note

Mummy Mummy you got to look at the stage!

I see music
On the stage
In the audience
All around this beautiful place
A singer sings so angelically
Her voice brings the crowd together so poetically

Beautiful Poem my dear!
Anara's Mom stated gently as she was so moved by Anara's soft words.

"Okay, two more spots to go, Mummy!" Anara declared, her voice filled with both weariness and unwavering enthusiasm. She was determined to show her Mom every place where she imagined music to be.
"We are off to the aquarium!" Anara exclaimed, her eyes sparkling with anticipation.
"I've never been to a musically inspired aquarium! This is just wonderful!" Anara's Mom exclaimed, sharing in her daughter's excitement. They embarked on their adventure to the aquarium, ready to discover the magical melodies that awaited them amidst the colorful underwater world.

I see music in all the jelly fishes
Swimming around, singing aloud
In all the colors, and bubbles
I see music, inside this tank
Fluttering around like confetti thrown up and down

"Mummy, did you think you would see some elephants today?" Anara asked, her voice filled with wonder.

"I didn't think I was going to a garden, a carnival, or a farm either! Another pleasant surprise on your beautiful melodic trail!" Anara's Mom exclaimed, marveling at the unexpected surprises they had encountered along their journey.

"Yes! Look, Mummy!" Anara exclaimed with excitement, pointing towards the magnificent elephants standing tall and majestic in front of them. They stood in awe, captivated by the grandeur of these gentle giants, and the melodies of the world seemed to blend harmoniously with the presence of these extraordinary creatures.

I see music in the jungle
In the monkey, the elephant and the parakeets
Singing with a bee, a lion and a goat
Telling me, let's go for a ride on this house boat!
Don't you see? Mummy
It's loud, it's soft
But most of all
Music....It's always in my heart
Floating, floating
Like a Bumble Bee
Singing like a lark.

So Anara's Mom enthusiastically responded,
"Yes I do my sweet heart!
Music is always in you
Floating and fluttering
Inside and out
Keep Singing, and humming
And remember
There is always a song to listen to
No matter how Soft or loud!"
Welcome to PianoPark

Anara's smile widened, and she beamed with pure glee. Overflowing with happiness, she wrapped her arms around her Mom in a tight, loving hug. In that moment, their hearts were filled with immense joy and gratitude for the magical journey they had experienced together.

The End

CRAFT TIME!: UNLEASH YOUR CREATIVITY!
IT'S YOUR MOMENT TO ADD COLORS. EMBELLISHMENTS.
AND FORGE A PATH USING THE POWER OF YOUR IMAGINATION! ENJOY!

# A little about the Author...

Nisha Thayil Manglani is an extraordinary woman who wears many hats. She is a loving wife and mother of two beautiful girls, a Licensed Clinical Social Worker, a Psychotherapist, and a classically trained singer. When her second daughter arrived and the world was in the midst of the Covid-19 pandemic, Nisha embarked on a creative adventure that led her to write and illustrate "Anara's Melodic Trail", a captivating children's book.

Throughout her life, Nisha has always felt the magical presence of music. Whether she was sitting, reading, contemplating, or cherishing moments with her family, melodies filled her heart. It was this deep love for music and the inspiration she found in her loved ones that propelled her to create the enchanting world of "Anara's Melodic Trail". Through this book, Nisha hopes to ignite the imaginations of her readers, encouraging them to dream fearlessly and explore the boundless possibilities that lie within the pages.

In the process of illustrating this delightful book, Nisha chose to use simple store-bought crayons. Inspired by her daughters' love for coloring and their imaginative use of crayons, Nisha embraced a motto: "You don't need fancy tools to create, color, and let your imagination soar. You can use whatever you have around you to bring it to life". By sharing this approach, Nisha hopes to inspire her daughters and readers alike, teaching them that dreaming, imagining, and creating limitlessly is the key to unlocking a world of endless possibilities.

Nisha Thayil Manglani's passion for music, her dedication to her family, and her belief in the power of imagination shine through the pages of "Anara's Melodic Trail". Join her on this whimsical adventure, and let your own imagination take flight!